Huli

by

JN Goulet

Ancient China is a land filled with gods and legendary creatures; before unified China and the separate empires, a powerful kingdom was nearly brought to its knees by a single creature of mischief.

In desperation, the emperor summons a priest.

"Priest, my kingdom is in peril from this monster. Disease and disasters are destroying my

people. Deadly weapons are useless against this thing. I need your help. I am willing to try anything to save my subjects." the emperor implores.

"My Emperor, the most I can do is pray to the Gods for help. Whether they help or even hear me is up to them. The only promise I can give is I will pray for help." says the priest Lie Jie.

Returning to his temple Lie Jie begins to pray to the Gods; not one God, but all of them throughout the night.

In the realm of Gods, one hears Lie Jie's plea for help. Lie Gong, God of thunder, who punishes evil-doers, humans, and demons.

Looking down upon the world, Lie Gong sees the root of the problem. A spirit fox called Huli Jing is terrorizing the people.

As a spirit fox, Huli Jing has lived for thousands of years. She is white with eight equally white tails with hints of red on their tips. Unlike a regular fox, Huli stands at a height twice the size of a wolf.

Her distaste for humans grew more over the centuries as the population grew.

The God Lie Gong finds Huli Jing in a field filled with dead cattle, which is why they are deceased.

"Huli Jing!" Lie Gong calls out, and Huli turns to where she hears the voice. "Cease your actions, or I will punish you!" Lie Gong commands.

As a fox spirit, Huli commands excellent power, but she is dwarfed by the presence of Lie Gong, knowing he could kill her in an instant.

"I will cease for the moment. While my power will continue to grow, yours will wane in time." Huli tells Lie Gong.

"Beware your words, Huli Jing. I am here to stop your meddling with the humans; continue; it will cost you your life." Lie Gong warns Huli.

A moment in a deity's point of view is not one or two years; it is more like thousands of years. Huli stops terrorizing the human population. She sleeps like an animal; for her, she wakes several thousand years in the future, the year 2022.

Chapter 1

The year is 2022 in China; in Jainca county, there is a small Buddhist temple, and in that temple resides a single monk whose tranquil life is about to be shaken by events.

"Delun Bao, have you heard the news?" One of the people

from the village asked him. "I do not hear much of anything. As the temple priest, I spend much of my time praying and keeping up with repairs. What has happened?" Delun Bao asked.

"There was an explosion at the military base to start; not long after, the livestock in the area began dying. At first suspected, dangerous chemicals were the cause.

Now several homes have mysteriously caught on fire. The military has no explanations of these events."

"Mr. Sung, take me to the nearest burnt home; maybe, I can

discover what is causing these disasters." Delun Bao says.

Arriving at a farmhouse, the monk Bao is perplexed by the burnt home, and the chickens housed several feet away. The building burnt to ash, and the chickens looked like they died where they were standing.

Bao starts walking around the burnt building in an outgoing circle, examining the ground.

"Venerable Bao, what are you searching for on the ground?" Mr. Sung asked. "I do not know. I hope to find a clue that could lead me in the right direction," says Bao. Continuing his search,

Bao stops to examine a set of footprints.

"Mr.Sung, are there any wolf's in the area?" Bao asked Sung. "There have not been wolves in this area in years," Sung tells him.

"Without wolves, this is a substantial wolf-like animal footprint.

I wish to examine another burnt home or animal death." Bao insisted.

"The next place is a field filled with dead cattle. It is three miles away from here." Sung tells Bao. "We should hurry; I do not wish to travel at night," says Bao. "As you wish, venerable Bao."

At the site of the dead cattle, Bao discovers the same large animal tracks. "Mr.Sung, I have seen enough. Please take me back to my temple." Bao says. "Do you know what is causing these deaths?" Sung asked. "I am not certain; I will have to pray for guidance," Bao tells Sung.

Delun Bao prays to his God for help at his temple in fear that whatever is causing the fires and animal deaths is spiritual.

No sooner finished praying, a large wolf-like creature, but not a wolf, twice the size, white, with multiple tails in flames, confronts Bao.

"Monk, it was foolish of you to pray for help; you will lose your life." the creature tells Bao.

"Huli Jing! You will not harm the priest!" Lie Gong tells her.

"You can warn me all you want; I have my ninth tail, and you are significantly weaker since the last time we met. Your time has passed, old God. You cannot harm me." Huli tells Lie Gong.

"You should consider yourself lucky my time has passed. This God the priest prayed to, requested me to deal with you with a little help. The Gods of this time are much more gentle. I cannot kill you, but I can do

this." Lie Gong says, snapping his fingers.

In a split second, Huli disappears. "What have you done to her?" Bao asked Lie Gong. "Your God wishes for her to appreciate the humans of this world. She will have a second chance. Though I do not think she will like what is in store for her, you should not have any more problems with her." the deity explains to Bao before vanishing.

Chapter 2

Orlando, Florida, life in an amusement park is very different from outside. The city is infested with crime and has an understaffed police force.

Gangs and violence control many streets at night, the most significant and violent is the Po Mou gang, whose leader is Angel Montebello; with over a hundred members, most of the streets are under his control.

Living in a drug-infested city is Scott Glassman, an ex-con trying to start a new life working in a convenience store; to his surprise, no one has robbed it.

It helps that he stays clear of the gangs and keeps to the side streets when he goes home.

"Scott, have you tallied the cash draw?" "Yes, I have Mr. Bilx," Scott replies. "You can go. I'll lock up."Mr.Bilx tells Scott.

Scott's walk home is interrupted by officer O'Malley. "Hold on for a second, Glassman." "Yes, officer O'Malley?" says Scott. "How's it going?" O'Malley asked. "I'm making ends meet," replies Scott. "I'm glad to hear that; typically, I would give you a hard time as an ex-con.

I know you don't hang with the gangs, and you're keeping yourself clean from the drugs. So I want to thank you for your effort." says O'Malley.

"I'm trying my best. I served my time; now I want a new life." Scott says. "I wish you luck and stay safe," says O'Malley.

Walking home, Scott receives a call from his sister Brenda. "Hi, Bren, what's up?" "How are you feeling today?" his sister asked. "I'm doing fine. You don't have to check up on me." "I'm not. I'm inviting you to dinner tomorrow. Are you interested?" Brenda asked. "Dinner sounds nice. What time?" says Scott.

"How does seven sound?"
"Seven it is." replies his sister.

Scott's mood perks up at having a home-cooked meal until she turns the corner, where he sees a large group of the Po Moe gang standing at the corner. Not wanting to confront them, Scott decides to cut through a small dark alley filled with trash and an eerie feeling.

Scott was expecting to find a homeless person or two sleeping in the alley when he noticed a faint light ahead of him; not wanting to disturb whoever was sleeping, he silently walked towards the glow not to wake whoever was sleeping.

When he approached the box, he didn't find a bum sleeping but an unusual-looking woman. She had no clothing on her body, Asian descent, then it got strange; with her shoulder black length hair, a pair of extra redfish brown ears on her head that did not match her hair; next was her butt, there's a fluffy reddish-brown tail.

Scott could not believe what he was looking at; he decided to try and wake the woman.

"Hey Miss, it's not safe here." Then, gently shaking her, Scott tells the woman. He gets no response from the woman. At first, he thought the ears and tail

were a prop; with closer examination, Scott discovers they are part of the woman's body.

"Lady, I don't know what you are; if I leave you here, your troubles will worsen with the company this area has for neighbors," Scott says.

Removing his shirt to put on the woman, Scott has to find a way to get her to his apartment without attracting any attention.

Living close to a crappy neighborhood with little to no street lights and nighttime gives Scott a decent chance of getting the woman to his apartment without getting noticed.

Once in his apartment, Scott lays his unusual guest on his bed.

"Let's cover you up while I decide what to do with you and dinner," Scott tells himself.

Chapter 3

Scott was pleasantly surprised by the woman's weight when he lifted her in his arms; she may top 90 pounds soaking wet, under five feet tall.

Getting the woman to his apartment unnoticed was still challenging; Scott had to wait for bystanders to walk clear several times.

Laying his guest in his bed, Scott covers her before going to his kitchen to cook up frozen patties on his George Foreman griller.

Taking the frozen patties from his freezer, Scott reaches for a knife to split the hamburgers.

Suddenly, Scott feels someone jumping on his back, screaming profanities. Dropping the knife, Scott struggles to get the crazed woman from his back.

Throwing her over his shoulder, Scott stands away from the woman.

"Relax! I will not harm you," shouts Scott. The woman stares at him with angry eyes as she grabs the knife on the counter. "I would not do that if I were you," he tells the crazed woman. She

ignores Scott's warning lunging at him.

As an excombat veteran, it is nothing new for Scott having people attack him with a knife. Unfortunately for the woman, she is disarmed and then knocked unconscious.

Scott feels something warm run down his chest with the woman lying on the floor. It's his blood; At first he thought he was cut, he realized she had bitten him.

Before doing anything, restraining whatever that woman is comes first. He doesn't need a repeat performance from her.

Securely strapped and gagged to a chair, Scott tended to his shoulder, then continued with his dinner.

The smell of the burgers cooking wakes his guest; she tries to scream and brake her bonds.

Calmly, Scott turns to the woman eating his burger.

" I can see you're pissed. Your black eye is getting even for my shoulder. Are you willing to listen to me?" Scott asked.

The woman's eyes sneered at Scott as she attempted to shout at him. "It looks like you're not ready," Scott says as he continues to eat.

The aroma of the greasy burger does not go unnoticed by Scott's guest; her rants subside as her drool oozes through the gag.

"Are you ready to talk? If you are, I'll give this to you." Scott tells the woman showing her the burger.

Her eyes are still red with anger; she stares at Scott. "I guess that close enough to yes, I'll get out of you."

Removing her gag, an assortment of profanities rolls from the woman's mouth. As a serviceman, Scott has heard his fair share of cuss words; what was coming from her mouth even surprised him.

In mid-sentence, Scott shoves a burger into the woman's mouth.

"Shut up and eat it," Scott tells her.

The woman's disposition begins to change as she chews the burger. Then, removing the burger from her mouth, Scott opens a can of coke to give her to wash down what's in her mouth.

"Much better," Scott says to the woman. She nods her head she is.

"My name is Scott Glassman, and you are?" "I am Huli Jing." replies the woman.

"My next question is; Those ears and tail are not fake. What are you?" Scott asked.

"Tail? My tails are missing! What did you do to them?" Huli says. "I didn't do anything to

your tails. A single tail is a way I found you." Scott tells Huli.

"That bastard God Lie Gong did this to me! I will make him pay! for this disgrace.

I am a spirit fox and am not from this land to answer your question. Now release me from these bindings!" insisted Huli.

"I never said I would release you," replies Scott. "You filthy bastard! I will kill you!"

"Talk like that is why you're not let loose," says Scott. "Why does my face hurt?" Huli asked. "That would be because you have a black eye I gave you," Scott tells Huli. "How is it that you can hurt me? A human should not be able

to do so." "I could be because whoever sent you here changed you. If you want me to set you free, we need to come to an understanding.

Chapter 4

"You say a God sent you here. If he or she did, you must have done something to piss them off. Where you are now is a dangerous place to be. Life is cheap to certain people.

I'm guessing your homeland is someplace in China. You won't travel back there soon as the world is now.

If I can hurt you, so can others. Two things need to change before you are set free. First, those ears and tail need hiding ."

"What is the other issue?" Huli asked. "Your shitty attitude needs to stop. It could get us killed." arrogantly, Huli replies. "Why should my attitude be a problem?"

"Humans in this neighborhood do not take kindly to loudmouth's," Scott stressed.

"Why should be concerned about humans? They mean nothing to me."Huli says. "You should be a concern. You're practically human yourself."

"If I give my word to be less boisterous, will you release me?" Huli requested.

"If I do, remember this; you can run away; I won't stop you.

People outside this place will sell you or use you for their pleasure. Neither is very pleasant." Scott warns Huli.

"I understand. What I do not know is why you befriended me?" Huli asked. "I have seen enough horror in my life. If the wrong class of people found you before me, you would have become part of the ugliness.

I didn't care what you were; I wanted to keep you clean."

Scott cuts the tie wraps holding Huli to the chair.

"You're free. What do you want to do?" Scott asked her. "Can I continue eating what you fed me?" Scott smiled. "Here. You

can wash it done with this." Scott gives Huli a can of coke.

Scott's cell phone rings. He can tell it's his sister calling him. He forgot about her invitation to dinner with all the excitement,

"Hi, Bren." "I thought you were coming over for dinner." his sister says. "I'm sorry. I had an unexpected company stopover." Scott tells his sister. "Is it the dangerous type?" Bren inquired. "I wouldn't say she's dangerous, but a handful," Scott answered. "Bring her along. I cooked plenty of food." Bren suggested.

"That may be somewhat difficult since the only clothes I gave her are the ones she wears.

I found her like a lost puppy unconscious in an alley with no clothes." Scott says to his sister.

"You had better use caution when with your statements. I am not the family pet!" Huli shouts.

Bren laughs, hearing Huli over the phone. "Bring her anyway. I might have some clothes for her to wear." "I don't know," says Scott. "What is wrong with me?" Huli shouts. Scott looks at her, pointing to her ears and tail. "Oh... Is this better?" Scott watches as her ears and tail disappear. "how come you didn't tell me you can do that?" said Scott. "You never asked, idiot!" replied Huli.

"It looks like you will have company for dinner. See you in a half-hour." Scott tells his sister.

"If you're coming with me, we must set some ground rules and a story. First, you are not a spirit fox but a woman with memory loss. I found you, and you don't know how you got here.

Second, do not wander away from me. We will be taking a bus to travel to my sister. Do not speak to strangers. Attracting attention from the wrong people can be unhealthy. I stayed safe by not getting noticed."

The bus trip to Scott's sister's home was uneventful most of the way. Once Scott had to remind

Huli not to insult the youngster dancing to his music on headphones, he apologized for her rudeness.

"Remember what I told you about keeping what you are a secret." Scott reminded Huli before knocking on his sister's door.

Chapter 5

"Scott, how are you and your friend doing? Please come in; dinner is still hot." Bren greets her brother.

"I'm fine. Bren, this is Huli Jing. Huli, this is my sister Brenda." Scott introduced. "Please follow me, Miss Jing. I have some clothes you can try on. You must be traumatize from your experience." Bren says. "It was a shock," said Huli.

"Scott, you can set up the table while Miss Jing and I do what we

have to do for clothing," Bren tells her brother.

A couple of minutes into setting the table, Scott hears his sister calling for him.

"Little brother can come into the bedroom for a moment. I need your opinion." O.k. I'll be right there." he replies.

"Yes? What do you need?" Scott asked as he walked into the bedroom. "Can you explain what I'm looking at?" his sister says as she steps out of the way for Scott to look at Huli.

In the summer dress stands Huli with her ears and tail in plain sight to see.

Angry, Scott walks up to Huli, grabbing hold of one of her ears. "You stupid fox! Why did you not take my advice?"

"Ow! release my ear! Why should I listen to a human? You are hurting me! Let go of my ear!" Huli shouts. "Shut up and sit down!" Scott tells Huli.

"Scott, whoever she is, stop hurting her!" Bren says. "Fine. I will tell you if you want to know what Huli is." Scott says. "I can speak for myself. I do not need you to do so." Huli tells Scott.

"O.k., Huli, who are you?" Bren asked her. Proudly Huli replies. I am a nine-tail spirit fox." "Tell her the rest," Scott commented.

"Your sister does not need to know anymore," Huli says.

"Sis, I'll fill you in on the rest. Huli is a mythical creature who is very naughty. From what I discovered, this is punishment. Henceforth the human-looking woman you see before you, with most of her powers stripped away.

I found her lying unconscious in an alley." Scott explains.' "Scott finished setting up the dinner table and take dinner from the stove; I need to have a conversation with Huli," Bren says.

"Why should I listen to you?" Huli says. "You're correct about

listening to me, but you will hear what I say.

My brother does not put his life on the line for strangers. You're wrong thinking your ears and tail make you different. Did my brother give you that black eye?" Bren asked. "He did," Huli replied. "Why?" "I attacked him with a knife." "You're lucky he didn't kill you," Bren tells Huli.

"You're brother smells of death. His soul, it is stained with blood," states Huli. "You are correct about his soul. Scott has taken many lives; that's what happens when you're in a war.

The scars of the innocent do the most damage. Scott returned as a damaged person. He has made mistakes that cost him. Ask yourself why did he help you? Why are you so special? You won't find the answer admiring yourself in the mirror. Time and the right circumstances will show you. Enough talk, let's eat; I'm hungry."

"Food's on the table; serve yourself," says Scott. "How does she look? Except for her height and chest size, my dress will do until you get Huli some proper fitting clothes." Bren tells her brother.

Scott almost broke out in laughter when he saw Huli

looking in the neck opening with a frown.

Asian women, in general, do not have much up top. Compared to Bren's D cup, Huli flat A is depressing.

"Miss Jing, I wouldn't worry about what you don't have; my brother will not judge you for it," Bren tells Huli. "I do not need his judgment or opinion to ease my mind." Huli states. "That's enough, Sis; let's eat," Scott says.

For the remainder of the evening, Huli was silent until exiting the bush near Scott's home.

Chapter 6

"Shit!" cried Scott. "What have I done?" Huli asked. "Nothing. We will have company when we get off the bus. Do not speak to them if confronted." Scott tells Huli.

"Glassman, I haven't seen you lately. Where have you been hiding?" "Work and sleep, Cho, that's all I do," replied Scott.

"Who is this beauty from my homeland accompanying you?" Cho asked Scott. "Her name is

Huli. She's staying with me." Scott explains to Cho.

With a grin, Cho speaks to Huli in Chinese. "Huli replies likewise. "You bitch! I'll gut you!" Cho takes out his knife.

Scott stands between Huli and Cho. "Hold it, Cho! There is no need for a knife. If Huli offended you, I will punish her. As you can see, she has a black eye. Her mouth tends to get her in trouble. What did she say that upset you?" Scott asked.

"Never mind. I'll let it slide this time. Make sure that bitch gets a slap for me when you get home." Cho tells Scott. "It's a promise," Scott says.

Once in his apartment, Huli confronts Scott about punishing her. "If you think of hitting me again, you had a better sleep with your eyes open," Huli warns Scott.

"It depends what he and you said to each other," Scott says.

"That idiot suggested that I be his sex slave." "How did you reply?" Scott inquired. "I told him he was a disgrace to women because his penis is as flat as my chest."

Scott begins to laugh out loud. "I do not see what is so funny about my chest size." Huli states.

"I'm not laughing about your chest; you told him his dick was

flat. You embarrassed him more than he was angry. That was the reason why he let us go."

Scott flicks Huli's nose with his finger. "What was that for?" Huli asked. "Punishment for doing something hazardous. Don't do that again.

It doesn't matter if you have a set like my sister on your chest. I'll judge you by what is behind that perky set."

"Why are you so frightened by others? Standing between that man and me, I sensed fear in you. I could say you are a coward; your sister told me you were a soldier which leads me to think otherwise." Huli states.

"My sister talks too much," Scott says. "You smell of death. How many lives have you taken?" Huli asked. "Too many of those who are deserving and those who are not," Scott replies. "How many of them not deserving did you kill?" "One is too many. No more questions; you can sleep on the bed, and I'll be on the couch.

Tomorrow is my day off; you and I will be going to the Salvation Army store," Scott tells Huli.

"Salvation Army? Are you buying a weapon?" Huli says. "No. The Salvation Army fights against poverty and the

desperate who are in need. I'm not the richest person around. The money I make working is enough to pay my rent and the necessities. You need more clothes; the Salvation Army is where to get used clothing. That's where most of my clothes are purchased. Gets some sleep; we'll take the early bus to get there in the morning,"

Chapter 7

Scott rises from his couch before Huli wakes from an uneventful night's sleep.

Knocking on the bedroom door, Scott calls to Huli.

"Miss Jing, it's time to get up; breakfast will be ready in minutes. do you hear me?" "I hear you," she replied.

"What is this?" Huli asked, staring at her plate. "It's called bacon and eggs; dig in. No fingers; use the fork," insisted

Scott. Huli sneers at Scott as she picks up the fork.

The bus trip to the Salvation Army store was non eventful; there was no one on the bus for Huli to antagonize.

Entering the store, you can see a variety of people shopping; a mother with children, bums, to well-dressed people.

"Let's get you some clothes; First undergarment, then the rest," Scott says.

Immediately Huli senses the mood of the people shopping. "What is wrong with these people?" Huli asked Scott. "What do you mean?" replied Scott. "There is a feeling of dread and desperation that hangs over them," Huli says.

"If there is, it's because they are struggling to survive. Unlike you, humans need food and clothing to live. This place gives them hope in many ways; not only in the products they buy but also in having a conversation with some having similar problems.

I have wanted to ask you; since you can speak English, can you read and write it?" "I am versed in many languages," replies Huli. "Good. I want you to start searching through these bras for your size. The letter you need to look for on the tags is this, A" Scott instructs Huli.

"I cannot," Huli replied. "If you want clothes, you're going to have to help. It is not the time to be stubborn," Scott tells Huli.

"I am not being stubborn! I am cursed," Huli tells Scott. "Cursed? Did the god who sent you here make you illiterate?" Scott inquired. "No. I am blinded; I cannot read the small letters. It is a blur to me," Huli explained.

It takes everything Scott has not to laugh at Huli's predicament.

"Can you see letters clearly at a distance?" asked Scott. "I can,"

replied Huli. "Follow me," says Scott.

Huli follows Scott to a bin filled with used prescription reading glasses.

"I don't think you were cursed, just made nearsighted," Scott says.

He removed his disabled veteran's identification from his wallet to show Huli.

"I want you to try different glasses on and tell me when you can see the small print clearly," Scott tells Huli.

As Scott holds his ID for Huli to read, he feels a tap on his shoulder. He turns. Sis, what are you doing here?" Scott asked.

"I knew you would take Huli here, so I decided to give you a hand. What's with the glasses?" Bren asked.

"It seems it's either a punishment or a joke; Huli was made nearsighted," Scott tells his sister.

Huli grabs Scott's hand, moving to and from her eyes. "I can read the small print with these glasses," says Hilu. Scott looks at the pair of glasses she chose. They are from the fifties, pink cat's eyes frames.

"Bren, how do they look on her?" Scott asked. Bren tilts her head, contemplating Huli's look. "I think they suit her personality.

Scott relax while I helped Huli with clothes. What's your budget?" Bren asked. "I planned on spending a hundred dollars," answered Scott. "A hundred dollars is more than enough to clothes Huli in this store," Bren tells her brother.

Used movies, books, furniture, and jewelry Scott browses; nothing changes in the store; he's shopped at the Salvation Army so many times there is rarely anything that catches his eye.

Today, in jewelry Scott pays attention to a necklace that has been on display for as long as he can remember. It's not glamorous or cheap fake diamonds; it's a simple chain with a small fox pendant.

Ten dollars is the price; Scott stares at it, thinking it would be a kind gesture for a particular guest living at his home.

"Scott, Huli is set for clothes. She should have enough clothes for all occasions, and it's under your budget," his sister tells him.

"Thank you, Bren. What do you have planned for the rest of your day?" Scott asked. "I still have to go to work. I stopped because I had the time, and I knew you needed the help.

Huli, I trust you can stay out of trouble. My brother has enough scars; he does not need anymore," Bren cryptically says. "I have to leave, little brother. I'll talk to you later," Bren says.

Chapter 8

"Thanks for your help, Sis. Huli, we'll go back to my place to drop off your clothes, then I'll give you a short tour of the neighborhood and where I work.

Before leaving Scott's apartment, Scott watches Huli perform a strange ritual; she starts licking herself.

"What are you doing?" Scott inquired. "I am cleaning myself," she replied. "This won't do. You are not a fox; humans take

showers," Scott states. "This way is fine with me," Huli says.

"Follow me," says Scott. "Why?" Huli says. "Humor me," Huli follows Scott to the bathroom, where he instructs her how the water works and where the soap and shampoo are.

Huli stares at Scott, "It does not mean I will take a shower," Her snub expression gets one reaction from Scott.

Grabbing her, she pushes Huli into the shower, then turns on the water.

"Let me out of here, you filthy human!" Huli cried out. "As long as you are a human, you wash as one. Now that your clothes are

wet remove them and use the shampoo and soap on the shelf.

When finished, you can choose what you want to wear. I'll shower next," Scott tells Huli.

Scott didn't need to shower; he decided to take one so Huli didn't feel out of place.

Scott hears the water run in the shower for ten minutes before Huli calls out. "I am finished. I smell like flowers," "Did you rinse yourself?" Scott asked. "I did. I am not ignorant of human ways," Huli tells Scott.

I'll shower once you get your clothes on," Scott shouts.

Huli waits in the living room for Scott to finish showering.

Scott steps from the bathroom with his pants on. "Give me a couple of minutes to finish getting dressed," says Scott. Huli looks at Scott's scared upper body.

"Did you die?" Huli says. "If you infer about my scars, I came close," Scott tells her.

"Your soul smells of blood. Are those scars the reason?" Huli asked.

"If you smell blood on my soul, the scars have nothing to do with it. The wrong end of an explosion caused those scars.

Too much killing and death are what you're smelling on me. How about you? How many deaths have you caused? You are here as a punishment," Scott stated.

"I may have caused a few humans to pass away. I lost count over the centuries . If I killed humans, I never considered them important,"

"That kind of thinking is what got you in trouble. Humans may not have incredible powers like you, but they are generally worth some respect. I grant you that some humans are trash. Even trash gets a second chance in life.

Are you ready to take a walk? There's a fast food place not too far from here; I'll buy lunch,"

Scott says. "Lead the way," Huli replies.

One of the points of interest Scott shows Huli is the nightclub area. "Down this street is where most come to drink at night. It used to be a good place when you wanted to have a good time. Lately, this place has taken a dark and deadly path. Booze, drugs, and guns have made it dangerous to have fun," Scott tells Huli.

Walking from a side street, Scott sees officer O'Malley staring at him.

"Mr. Glassman!" "Yes, officer O'Malley," Scott replied. " If you're showing the young lady

the city, be cautious. Mo Poe is stirring up trouble. Try not to stay out too late at night. That pretty young woman you're with could attract the wrong attention," Officer O'Malley warned.

"I will keep that in mind, Sir. I already had a run-in with one of the gang," Scott says.

"Who the young woman's name at your side? I have never seen her in this neighborhood before," O'Malley asked.

"Officer O'Malley, this is Huli Jing. She will be living with me until she finds a place of her own," Scott explained.

"It's a pleasure to meet you, Miss Jing. I pray our city treats you well. You should consider yourself lucky; Mr. Glassman has taken you in. Orlando once was a good place to live," O'Malley tells Huli.

"I am beginning to think you are right about this human. I wish you a good day," Huli says to officer O'Malley.

Turning to Scott, Huli reminds him of her promised lunch. "I am hungry. Take me to a fast food place you mentioned," "O.k." "I will see you around, officer O'Malley," Scott says as Huli pulls Scott away.

Sitting on a bench, Scott watches Huli engulf her burger and fries.

"Your's are much better," Huli says, stuffing her face. "I'm glad you appreciate my cooking," replied Scott.

Chapter 9

Where the former library on Church Street once was, a group of people meet in the abandoned structure.

"Listen up! Angel has a few words to say before you leave." Cho shouts.

"Before you leave to run your areas, make sure your dealers don't get too careless. The cops are inept but not blind. We own some of the cops, not all of them. Especially O'Malley.

We have control of the city because we keep what we do a low profile. That includes killing. Make certain it goes through me before taking someone out. Killing someone with influence will bring outside people into the city. So before you leave, give Cho your tally, and if you need more cocaine to sell," Angel instructs his men.

Angel and his lieutenant Cho are still in the building; they get down to business, counting their drug sales and other crimes they make a profit from.

How are today's profits looking?" Angel asked Cho as he finished counting. "Not bad.

Sales are slacking in the little Vietnam section," Cho informed his boss. "Is there a reason for the lack of sales?" Angel asked. "Some of our clients are finding it difficult paying up," Cho says.

"They must be having a lack of courage. I want you to choose one of our non paying customers and give him some courage by breaking his legs and arms. Don't kill him. When finished, call for an ambulance. Our non paying business associates will get the message," Angel instructs Cho.

"Angel, why do you put up with Glassman? I noticed you never robbed the store where he

works," Cho asked. "He's an ex-con, one of those high profile persons I spoke of; Glassman is very friendly with O'Malley."

Angel explained that an honest police officer who is personally close to Glassman could be dangerous to us," Angel explained.

"For now, he's off-limits. What if he begins to cause problems for us?" Cho asked. "We're all expendable," replied Angel.

Chapter 10

"Huli, This is where I work. Can you remember how to get here from my apartment?" Scott asked her. "I can find my way here if needed," she replied. "Good. You will be on your tomorrow. I will leave plenty of food to eat while I'm gone. If you need help, you'll know where to find me," Scott says.

"I will be fine, as long there is food. How long will you be gone?" Huli asked. "Eight hours. Seven in the morning to three in the afternoon. I'll show you more about the city when I return from

work. Since you're from China, I know a good and cheap Chinese restaurant to eat at,"

"Do not presume I will like that type of food because it originates from my homeland," Huli tells Scott.

"You're saying that in all those years living in China, you never tasted the food the people eat," "I am a spirit fox. I do not need food to survive, nor hungered for it," "We'll find out tomorrow if you like Chinese," Scott says.

That evening, Scott lays out blankets and a pillow on his couch to sleep.

"Why do you continue to sleep out here? There is plenty of

space on the bed with me, "Huli states. "No, it's too dangerous," Scott states. "I promise not to harm you," says Huli. "That's not the danger I meant. It's safer on the couch, now go to sleep," Scott tells Huli.

Setting his alarm to wake two hours early before work, Scott prepares lunch for himself and Huli before leaving.

Quietly, Scott leaves for work, trying not to wake Huli.

Arriving a little earlier than usual, the store manager comments about Scott's arrival.

"You're here early; is something going on at home?" Scott's boss Bilx asked. "You

could say that. I have a guest staying over, and I'm not sure when she will be leaving," Scott tells his manager.

"Is she Asian and around five feet in height?" Mr.Bilx says. "Yes. How do you know she's Asian and her height?" Scott asked.

"Someone fits that description standing outside the store," Scott is told.

Turning to see who's standing, Scott takes a deep sigh.

Holding the door open, Scott calls to Huli. "Come in," "You left me alone," Huli tells Scott. "I did tell you I was working today, and I left prepared meals for breakfast and lunch on the table," Scott explained to Huli.

"I know. I had eaten those meals already," "If you did, why are you here?" Scott asked. "I do not want to be alone," "You can't stay here. I have to work," Scott says.

"Mr.Glassman, is this the guest you spoke of earlier?" "Yes, Mr.Bilx," "Introduce her to me, Mr.Glassman," "Huli Jing, this is the store manager Tao Bilx.

"Miss Jing, I know Mr. Glassman is a good and dedicated worker; if you are living with him, I could say the same about you.

How would you like a job here at the store? It does not pay much, but you will be Mr. Glassman most of the day," Bilx offered.

"What type of work will I be doing?" Huli asked. "It will be hard work. Mr.Glassman will be behind the counter and you will be cleaning the toilets and moping the floors,"

Doing manual labor infuriated Huli, only to be calmed when Bilx offered a free meal for lunch from the store daily.

The smell of steamed hotdogs and pizza cooking in the oven was too tempting to resist.

It's the afternoon, Scott starts closing up the store. "Huli, I was impressed that you worked hard cleaning and eating. Two hotdogs, a sandwich with chips, and a large soda. Will you still have an appetite for Chinese after that lunch?" Scott says. "Do not worry, I will," Huli tells Scott.

"Once we lock up, we'll take the bus to little Vietnam. That's where we'll have dinner,"

Entering the restaurant, Scott and Huli are seated, the waitress hands Scott and Huli a menu.

Because many people who eat at the restaurant are Asian, the menu is in English and Chinese;

Huli speaks to the waitress in Chinese when selecting what she wants to eat.

Sitting at a table is an older woman who owns the restaurant. She picks up on Huli's conversation. Huli is speaking to the waitress, who happens to be her granddaughter. The owner of the restaurant listens to Huli and her dialect; it is one that she has not heard since she was a child. Then only the elderly of her childhood spoke it.

The older woman walks over to Scott and Huli and speaks to Huli in her native language.

The woman and Huli's conversation lasted for five

minutes or so. Not understanding, Scott could only read the woman's facial expressions to Huli. Scott sees fear in the woman's eyes for a split moment. The owner of the restaurant instructs her granddaughter that there will be no charge for their meal.

"Sir, my grandmother informed me you can order whatever you wish at no cost,"

"Immediately, Scott stands and bows, speaking to the old woman. "Please forgive Miss Jing if she has threatened you," implored Scott.

"Relax, Mr. Glassman; Miss Jing has not threatened me. The

free meal is to honor her. I know who she is. I should apologize for speaking to her in a language you did not understand. I am Mrs. Lou." explained to Scott.

"Grandmother, who is this woman?" "She is a very old friend," the grandmother replied, confusing her granddaughter.

Chapter 11

"What did you talk about with Mrs.Bea?" Scott asked as he ate. "Reminiscing of her past. You do not have to worry about the woman giving away who I am. She does not have much life left in her. I give her one to three

days before she dies," Huli tells Scott.

"Did the woman tell you this?" Scott asked. "No. I sensed it when she walked up to me," Huli says. "Did you feel sorry for Mrs. Bea?" Scott asked. "I do not know if I felt sorry, more like comforting," Huli explained.

Scott reaches in his pocket for a small box. "I wasn't sure when to give this to you. What you did for Mrs.Bea was sincere. Now seems the perfect time,"

"What is this?" Huli asked. "Open it. Stuck as you are must be hard. I thought it might help relieve some of your anxiety," Scott tells Huli.

Huli opens the box and stares at the necklace with the small fox pendant.

"Why are you doing this?" Huli asked. "I don't know how long your punishment is going to last; when you do return home, you'll have something to remind you it was not all bad,"

"I wish you had not done this," Huli says. "If you don't like it, you can throw it away," Scott tells her. "I did not say I did not like it. I just wished you had not given it to me," Huli says with a troubled expression.

"Want me to help you put it on?" "I can do it when I am ready. Please allow me to finish

my meal peacefully," Huli tells Scott.

"I have to use the restroom. I will be back in a minute," Scott says.

Returning from the restroom, Scott notices a small trinket hanging from Huli's neck. Knowing It made her uncomfortable talking about it, he decides not mention he sees the necklace on her neck.

They finished their meal, and Scott thanked Mrs.Bea for her hospitality.

Once Scott and Huli leave, Wei Lin speaks to her grandmother. "Who is that woman grandmother? There is

something different about her."
"She is someone extraordinary, Lin. If and when she is willing, you will know who she is," Lin's grandmother replies.

Walking back to the bus stop, Scott catches from the corner of his eyes an unpleasant event happening. Some of Angel's men are dragging the store owner of a shop into an alley.

"Scott, what is wrong?" Huli asked. "I want you to stay here." Looking around, Scott finds what he's looking for; a piece of clothing tossed in a waste bin near the bus stop.

Following Angel's men into the alley, Scott uses the old shirt to conceal his face.

Unknowing to Scott, Huli does not listen to his advice; she follows him to the alley.

Huli watches Scott from the corner of the street. The timid man she knew was a farce. The three men are knocked unconscious before Angel's men can seriously harm the store owner. Huli finds it hard to believe what she has witnessed.

Scott departs as quickly as he arrives, taking hold of Huli's hand pulling her along.

"I thought I told you to stay put!" Scott tells her. "You are a

skilled warrior. Why do you hide under this facade of a coward?" Huli asked.

"I have seen people who become accustomed to killing; as you said, I have a tainted soul. The fear of becoming like those people lead me to drug addiction and prison.

Killing becomes easy when you have skills and start losing conscience. It took a lot of effort not to kill those men. If I'm not careful, I could turn out like you, with no regard for human life. Stay here; I have to do something with those men.

Next time I tell you to stay put, do it. I saved that poor shop owner; the reason I concealed my face was not to have the rest of the gang trying to kill me. If they had seen you, it would lead Angel and his shit heads to us. Please stop trying to get us killed," Scott insisted.

Chapter 12

The bus ride back to Scott's apartment is a solemn one for Huli. Too many conflicting emotions troubling her.

"Was it true saying you were lonely when I left you home?" Scott asked Huli. "I was," she replied.

"Tell me about where you live. Where in China do you consider home?" Scott asked. "The area you could say I come from is rural. There are a few farms scattered in the area with a temple the humans call Jainca,"

Huli says. "Have you lived there most of your life?" Scott asked. "As long as I can remember," Huli says. "It sounds like a quaint place to live," says Scott.

"You could say that it is quaint. The area has not changed much in the last thousand years. There is technology, but most humans keep life simple," "With luck, you return there to see it again. Scott remarked.

A week passed; Huli receives her first paycheck. "What do I do with this?"Huli asked Scott. "Since you don't have a bank account, Mr. Bilx will cash it for you," Scott says. With cash in her hand, Scott says. "You can spend it anywhere you wish," "I wish to eat at a Chinese restaurant," Huli suggested.

"You may have to wait on Chinese. The restaurant is closed due to a death in the family," Mr. Bilx informs Huli. "I'm sure Miss Jing can find someplace to spend her money," Scott says.

When Scott and Huli arrive home, someone familiar is waiting for them at his apartment. The waitress from the Chinese restaurant. "Miss Lin, I heard about your grandmother. Sorry for your loss. How may I help you?" Scott asked.

"May I speak to you and Miss Jing in private?" Mei Lin asked.

"Of course. Please come in," says Scott.

"Take a seat, Miss Lin. What is on your mind?" Scott inquired.

"My grandmother wrote this letter before she passed away. I wish to read it to you; then tell me what it means. Lin proceeds reading the letter.

"Mei Lin, I have lived a good life; my only regret is that I met someone extraordinary at the end of my time.

I pray you will meet this person when you are young, so you can cherish the wonder of knowing that such an exquisite person could exist. I give you my love Mei Lin. The next time we will meet will be in the next world."

Mei Lin stares at Scott and Huli. "What does this mean?" Lin asked.

"Miss Jing, what do you think? Should you?" Scott asked. Huli nods yes.

"Miss Lin, google Huli Jing's name on your cell phone," Scott suggested.

Lin types Huli's name; what comes up as a reply is the legend of a spirit fox and a cartoon picture of how she would look.

Staring at her cell, Lin says. "What does that have to do with Miss Jing?"

Looking up, Mie Lin stares at Huli's ears and tail. "You must be kidding me," Mei Lin states.

"I assure you, Miss Lin, these ears and tail are real," Huli tells her. "Can I touch them?" Lin asked. "Go ahead," replied Huli.

After stroking Huli's tail, Lin's following statement came as a surprise to Huli. "It's a bit underwhelming. I would have thought you'd look somewhat as the legends described,"

Scott lets out a chuckle. "Miss Jing is as she is because she made someone angry. Most of her powers are gone, and her ears and one tail are all she can do."

"You are finding my condition amusing. I do not," Huli scolds Scott.

"How did my grandmother discover who you are?" Lin asked Huli. "I told her. She deserved to know out of respect.

I do not know if you knew; your grandmother only had a few more days to live. I knew her time was short, so I revealed my identity to her. I wish I could have done more. But, because of the state of my power, I could not help her or show her my proper form.

From the letter she wrote, it was enough for her to pass on with a smile," Huli tells Mie Lin.

"So, Mie Lin, what are you going to do?"Scott asked her. "If you mean I will keep Huli Jing a secret, my lips are sealed," Lin tells Scott. "Thank you, Miss Lin," says Scott. "My grandmother requested that the two of you can eat free of charge from now on," Lin says.

Huli's eyes glow with excitement. "I thank you for the offer, but it won't be fair since Huli can eat more than a normal person. We'll pay. If you want, you can give us a discount," suggested Scott. "Can I touch your ears again before returning to the restaurant?" Mei Lin asked. Huli lowers her head for Lin to rub.

Mei Lin's heart beats faster as her fingers scratch behind Huli's ears. "That is enough. I am not a family pet. You should leave before it gets dark," Huli tells Lin.

Chapter 13

"What the hell happened? Where have you been?"Angel asked his men as they walked into the library. "We were knocked out and thrown in a dumpster. We woke up in a truck outside of town," one of Angel's men tells him. "I hope that old man you were supposed to lean on didn't do that to you," says Angel.

"It wasn't him. Someone jumped us when we were

working on him. Don't ask who it was; we don't know. Whoever it was, is skilled and very silent and had his face covered," Angel is informed.

"This is not good. If people start taking the initiative, it could pose a problem for me.   I'll have Cho look into the matter.

What I want from you and the others is to take a bath. You smell like shit," Angel insisted.

Later that day, Angel is discussing with his second in charge.

"Cho, I need you to look into this mystery hero who's getting involved in my business," "When I do find this hero, what do I

do?" Cho asked. When you find that person, inform me before doing anything. I will point out what happens to those who get in my way. Start with the old store owner our guys were collecting. He might know who saved his ass," Angel suggested.

Preparing for bed, Huli decides to speak to Scott about Mie Lin. "Scott, would you consider Miss Lin a fine woman from a human's perspective?" "I would say so from what I know of her and her looks. Why are you asking?" Scott inquired. "Oh... I thought she would be good for mating. Have you considered doing it with her?" Huli asked.

"No. Lin's not my type," "What is your type? Mei Lin's heart rate does race a little when she speaks to you, and you said she's a fine woman," "Huli, stop what your doing," "Only if you explain to me what type of woman you prefer. If you do not, I will let Mei Lin think you are interested in her," Huli threatens Scott.

Scott has had enough of Huli's foolishness. Pulling her into his arms, he kisses her. Caught off guard, Huli can only stare at Scott's eyes as her lips press against his.

A few seconds pass, and Scott's lips release their hold on Huli. "Conceded and annoying foxes are my type. It's time to go to sleep," Scott says.

Huli stands still in shock, then fear; she pounces on Scott, taking him to the floor.

"What did you do to me!!!" Huli cries out.

Looking into Huli's eye's filled with fear and confusion, Scott realizes what he has done to her.

Breaking her hold on him, Scott wraps his arms around Huli. "Forgive me, Huli; I didn't mean to upset you," Huli struggles to break away from Scott. "Release me! You cursed me," exclaimed Huli. "I didn't curse you. It could be worse if you don't let me help you,"

After several minutes of speaking to Huli, she calmed down enough for Scott to release his hold on her.

"Huli, listen to my voice; what you're experiencing, humans feel every day, we sometimes have trouble handling what's going through your mind. It must be worse for you because of who you are. Having feelings for someone can be scary. I'm just as scared as you. It's o.k. to be frightened; it's your heart protecting you.

I'm sorry for scaring you," "You should be, "Huli tells Scott. "I had no intentions of hurting you," Scott tells Huli. "You did not hurt me. The confusion I felt frightened me,"

"Huli, it looks like the longer you remain as a human, the more human emotions you will experience. Some will be more pleasant than others. I don't want you to be bashful if you're having problems understanding how you're feeling. I will always listen to what you say, whether it makes sense or not.

I have a bottle of cheap wine, a glass will help you, and I relax before going to sleep. We have to get up early to open the store," Scott says.

Throughout the night, one sleeps soundly and other lays awake, sorting out how she feels.

Scott and Huli arrive at the store; Mr. Bilx came a few minutes before to unlock the door.

"Are we ready to start another day?" Bilx says. "Scott replies he is, but Huli is silent as she walks past Bilx.

Into the day, Huli remain silent, Bilx comments to Scott.

"Mr. Glassman, has something happened? Miss Jing is quieter than normal," " I think Huli has some personal issues she is trying to understand. It's nothing to be worried about; she needs a

little time to think, that's all," Scott tells Bilx.

Into the afternoon, customers enter and leave the store; Huli still is in her silent mood.

A mother and child enter the store to purchase some food. Standing at the register, the mother and child place their items on the counter.

Huli is staring at Scott as he rings up the customer's purchase.

Huli's eyes brighten, and her expression perks up. She walks up to Scott, places her hands on his face, and kisses him in front of the customers.

"Scott, I have decided that I enjoy kissing you. You may do it as you please," Huli says.

The child's mother is smiling and three shades of blush on Scott's face. "Huli, it's nice to know, but this is not the time for revelations. We'll talk about this later," says Scott. "That is fine with me. I will look forward to our conversation," replies Huli.

Chapter 14

"Why will you not kiss me again? I said I enjoyed it," Huli tells Scott. "You're too whimsical," "What is that supposed to mean?" Huli asked. "Liking is not enough; you're a heart breaker.

I understand you're adjusting well to having human emotions, the most important one, and you're a long way off. Until you know what I just said, no more," Scott insisted.

There's a knock on Scott's door. "Who could that be?'Huli

asked. "I don't know. Look through the peephole and find out," Scott says.

Huli looks through the peep. "It is the policeman you spoke to the other day," Huli says. "Let him in. He must have something important to discuss with me,"

"Officer O'Malley, what brings you here?" asked Scott. "Don't play coy with me, Mr. Glassman. Two days ago, there was an incident in the little Vietnam district off route 50.

Three of Angel's men found themselves miles away in a trash bin. No one saw or said anything; this time, it was for the better of the community.

Whoever this person is should know the Poe Moe gang is searching for this individual.

My fellow not-so-honest officers are searching for this person as well. However, I suggest this person does not harass Angel's men for his health.

Miss Jing, if you happen to see this person, try to keep him from getting shot," officer O'Malley suggested. "I will try," replied Huli.

"Miss Jing, I leave him in your hands. It would be a shame to find the only decent city resident dead," officer O'Malley says.

Officer O'Malley leaves after informing Scott of his predicament.

"Scott, why is the policeman warning you?" Huli asked. "Human kindness, I suppose. Huli, are there others of your kind?" Scott asked. I would not know. I assume there are others like me somewhere in the world. I have no interest in meeting with others of my kind. I prefer a solitary life."

Huli pauses when something comes to her mind.

" I noticed you are not calling Miss Jing. Is there a reason?" Huli asked. "If it upsets you, I can continue to address you,

Miss jing. I thought our friendship was at the point where I can speak to you less formally," explained Scott.

"I am not offended. It is pleasant when you address me as Huli; I will allow you to continue.

I am curious; you mention human kindness. You do not sound too sincere. Do all your cities have this effect on people?" Huli asked.

"It's not like the cities are the cause; the world, in general, is sick. Diseases, war, starvation, oppression, and lack of hope are killing this world.

You exist in a different world, so I wouldn't expect you to be concerned if the world is flushing itself down the drain," Scott says.

"I am not blind about the world; I feel it changes when something dramatic happens," Huli tells Scott.

"The world is becoming dark; the best I can do is give it a little light. That's why I got involved with those punks threatening the shop owner. I fear it will cost my life," Scott states.

Chapter 15

"Do not give me that dung about helping that person; from what I discovered, you rarely go out of your way to help anyone.

Why did you put your life in danger to help him?" Huli insisted, staring into Scott's eyes.

"I did it for you," replied Scott. "For me? That is ridiculous," says Huli. "You don't have to believe me, but that's why," Scott tells her.

"I do not believe you. You have other motives for doing what you did." Huli states.

"If you want to be a pain, I'll explain it so you can understand.

I'm not blind; you're here to learn. I won't tell you what. That's for you to find out. I risked my life for you to have a chance to go home. Your body is nice, but it's not your real one. I felt you're worth the risk," Scott says.

Scott's words give Huli her first taste of humility; the rest of the day, she's having difficulty shaking that feeling.

Forewarned, Scott is not aware Angel's subordinate Cho is hard at work trying to find out who's getting involved in his boss's business. Cho starts with the person Scott saved from having his legs broken.

"I swear I don't know who it was! Your men knocked me out before I could look at him. When I woke up, your men were gone, and the guy was gone as well," the store owner explained to Cho.

"You had better not hold anything back, old man. It won't be your legs you will lose," Cho warns the store owner.

"I remember seeing someone peeking into the alley," Cho's told. "Who?" "I do not know, but it was a woman," "A woman? Did you recognize her?" Cho asked. "She was too far away for

me to recognize," the store owner tells Cho. "That had better be all you know. If you find out who she or the guy is, inform Angel or someone working for him," Cho tells the store owner.

In fear, the old store owner nods he will.

At Bilx's store, Huli is about to experience human emotion that leaves her confused and angry with herself.

The scenario starts with a young woman entering the store.

"Hello," the young woman greets Scott. "Hello. How can I help you?" Scott asked. "The whole time the woman spoke to Scott, her eyes focused on Scott's

face. Speaking with an alluring voice, the woman tries to attract Scott's attention.

"Are your hours long here?" the woman asked Scott. "Some days are longer than others," replied Scott. "My nights are free. If you're interested, we could go for a drink sometime." the woman suggested to Scott.

"It's a nice gesture, but I have little time for myself. Thank you for the offer," Scott says. "Are you sure? I can promise you a pleasant evening." says the woman. "I'm sure," Scott replies.

The woman was about to continue her conversation when

it was interrupted by water rushing over her shoes.

"What the hell! Look what you have done to my new shoes!" the woman exclaimed to Huli.

"Forgive me. It was not intentional. I will clean your shoes for you." Huli says. "Never mind cleaning my shoes. Start with the floor so I don't slip and fall," the woman insisted.

Mr.Bilx leaves his office to see what the commotion is. "Miss, I will replace your shoes if you send me the cost. I'm sure it was an accident," Bilx says. "You will get the bill," the woman insisted as she stormed from the store.

Scott gives Huli a stern gaze. " I want to speak with you after you clean this mess," Scott tells her.

Away from the counter, Scott and Huli are having a heated discussion. "You did that on purpose," "What are you talking about?" Huli replied. "If you're going to act like an idiot, I will treat you like one.

When working, the customer is treated with respect, even if they do not do likewise. I suggest you keep your petty jealousy at home," Scott tells Huli.

"What makes you think I was jealous?" Huli says. "I saw the look on your face when that

woman was flirting with me," "I was not jealous!" insisted Huli. " If not, when she returns to have her new shoes paid for, you won't mind if I spend the day with her,"

Huli grabs hold of Scott's sleeve. "I will not let you," Huli states with a sneer.

"What I see in your eyes is old fashion possessive jealousy. I have no interest in dating that woman. But, as I said, my interest is in an immature fox who can be annoying. Do not mistake interest for commitment. You have a lot to learn about human emotions. When that woman returns, I expect you to

learn what humility is with a sincere apology," Scott insisted. Huli nodded; she understood.

Chapter 16

Mei Lin is no stranger to the seediness of her neighborhood. What was once an excellent place to live has become dangerous. She was taught well by her grandmother to observe her surroundings. The restaurant's security cameras and the windows allow her to survey the street without being noticed. Keeping aware of unwanted guests is a priority.

Lately, Mei Lin has noticed Angel's people harassing the store owners on the street more than usual. Speaking to one of the store owners, she discovers the reason why. Someone is searching for two people, a man, and a woman, who assaulted three of Angel's people.

It didn't take long for Mei Lin to figure out who they were looking for since the time and day consigns with Scott and Huli's visit.

Closing the restaurant early, Lin decides to pay another visit to Scott's apartment.

A knock on the door receives a curious eye in the door's peephole. "Scott, Mei Lin is here. Shall I open the door? She might have brought some food with her," Huli says. "Let her in, and do not pester her about food," Scott says.

"Hello, Mei Lin. Please come in," Huli greets her. "What can we do for you? Shouldn't you be running your restaurant?" Scott inquired.

"I came across disturbing news, which prompted me to close early.

I spoke to other store owners when I saw them harassed by the local thugs. Someone is searching for two people who tossed Angel's people in the trash bin. It happened about the time when you left my restaurant. I don't have to think too hard to discover who is responsible.

You don't have to worry about me, but someone will point Angel's people in the right direction," Mie Lin informs Scott.

"Miss Lin, if Angel's people confront you, I want you to tell them what they want to hear. You're not a good enough liar to fool anyone. I don't want you putting yourself in danger.

There are a few police officers that are still honest in this city. Officer O'Malley is one you can trust if someone starts pressuring you,"

"Miss Jing, is there something you can do about keeping Scott

out of trouble?" Lin asked. "Huli can't do anything in her current state. I'm doing what I can to keep her from causing a scene.

You should go home and don't attract any attention from Angel's people," Scott suggested.

"I will when the bus comes around in twenty minutes," Lin tells Scott.

"Why didn't you use your car to get here? It's getting dark and too dangerous to wait for the bus.

You can stay the night here. You can sleep with Huli and go home in the morning if she does not mind," Scott suggested.

"Miss Jing, is that o.k. with you?" Lin asked her. "I do not mind if you do not mind eating Scott's cooking. It is not up to your standards," Huli states.

"If you're allowing me to stay the night, I'll do the cooking. So let me see what you have in your fridge. Mei Lin rummages through Scott's fridge.

You're lacking a lot if you want a decent meal," Mei Lin tells Scott.

"Make a list, and I'll run to the corner store," Scott says.

With Scott hurrying to pick up ingredients for dinner, Huli uses the time to speak to Mei Lin privately.

"Miss Lin, would you consider me to be whimsical?" Huli asked. "I don't know. I've known you for only two days. Why do you ask?" Mei Lin says. "Scott will not let me kiss him again. He says I am too whimsical," Huli explained.

"You say he kissed you. How did you feel after kissing Scott?" Mei Lin asked. "Confused at first, then I wanted more. When I asked him to kiss me again, he refused,"

"If you want Scott to kiss you again, you'll need to learn what love is. It's not enough to physically touch him; you must want him from your heart. I don't know if you can feel that way.

You're not human," Mei Lin says. "You could be correct about not knowing what you described. To feel that is alien to me.

I suggested to Scott that you would be a good candidate for mating," Huli tells Lin. "What was Scott's reply?" Mei Lin asked.

"He said you were not his type," "Did Scott say who was his type?" Mei Lin asked. "He said he preferred an annoying, arrogant fox," Huli says. "Scott said that; there is hope for you yet. I think he's waiting for you to mature," Mei Lin tells Huli. "Mature; I'm thousands of years old," "Maybe it's not time which

determines maturity, but the experience. Living as a human is new for you. I would take one day at a time if I were you," Mei Lin suggested. "I will consider your advice. I hear Scott at the door. Please do not mention our conversation to him," Huli asked. "My lips are sealed,"

Chapter 17

"That was a wonderful meal. Did your grandmother teach you to cook?" Scott asked Lin. "She did. My mother passed away when I was young, so my grandmother cared for me. She taught me cooking to help me grieve and remember my mother in good way,"

"Your mother may have passed away when you were young; the time she raised you was enough to make you a good woman," Scott tells Lin.

Mei Lin's complexion blushes, and she is silent from Scott's comment.

It's getting late. If you need a nightgown, I'm sure Huli can lend you one of her's for the night," says Scott.

Huli and Mei Lin chatted a bit before falling asleep. In the morning, Lin speaks to Scott before she leaves.

"Huli is a little confused; you should spend quality time with her. I know you're not one to venture out at night, but it would help Huli if you take her out to one of the clubs to relax.

You don't have to close the bar, but spend a couple of hours around people enjoying themselves," Mei Lin suggested.

"I'll think about it. Thank you for spending some time with Huli. She may be a fox, but she's also a female. I'm sure you and she had some meaningful conversations together," Scott says. "Maybe we did, maybe we didn't. It's a secret. Have a good day, Mr.Glassman." says Mei Lin as she walks away.

"Did you and Mei Lin have any problems sleeping?" Scott asked Huli. "We slept fine. We should hurry to get ready for work. Mr. Bilx will be angry if we are late," says Huli. "Yea. Having Lin stay

over screwed up my schedule," replies Scott.

"Why are you smiling?" Huli asked. "I'm smiling because I'm happy and a little sad. You're becoming more human in your traits; I don't think that's how it should be. You're a spirit fox. It would be sad for the world to lose that part of you.

Let's change the subject; I'm taking Mei Lin's advice. You and I will spend the evening dancing after work. There are still one or two good nightclubs downtown," Scott suggested. "I do not know how to dance," Huli replies. "Don't worry; all you need to do is follow my lead," suggested Scott.

At nine o'clock in the evening, Scott gives Huli last-minute encouragement about her clothes before leaving to visit a nightclub.

"You look wonderful. There is no need to be so nervous. Neither of us is going to a ball. The place will be noisy and casual," Scott tells Huli.

"I do not like crowds; most of my life was spent in seclusion," Huli tells Scott. "You will be fine. Take my hand," says Scott.

Entering the night club Huli's senses feel that she's under attack by the loud music and the crowd's chatter. She tries to pull away from Scott's hand.

"Everything will be fine. It's o.k. to be a little frightened, especially when you're not used to this kind of environment. I'll order you a drink to calm your nerves,"

Once finishing her drink, Scotts notices Huli begins to relax. "Are you willing to give dancing a try?' Scott asked. I told you, I do not know how to dance." Huli stated.

"It's strange you not knowing how to dance," says Scott. "I'm a fox. Dancing is not part of my daily habits," Huli says.

"For someone who is supposed to be in tune with magic and nature, you would have figured out that music and the sounds of nature are similar.

The wind, animals, and the sounds of the forest sing a melody.

Take my hand. This music is a waltz; it should be easy for you to follow," Scott says.

The DJ plays an old tune. How deep is your love for the Bee Gees? Scott instructs Huli to wrap her arms over his shoulders as he wraps his arms around her waist. Holding her close, he says. "Listen to the melody, and I will do the rest,"

Resting her head on Scott's chest, Huli finds two things happening as she dances. First, she's moving to the song's rhythm.

With her sensitive hearing, one sound is drowning the noise of the nightclub; Scott's heartbeat.

The longer she listens to Scott's heart, the faster her's races.

When the song finished, Scott noticed Huli was breathing erratic as she looked at him.

"Huli, are you o.k.? You look a little flustered." Scott inquired. "I am fine," she replied. "We can take a break before dancing again," Scott says.

"I could use another drink," replies Huli. After a few more drinks and several dances, two hours have passed. Scott decides it's time to call it a night.

"Are you ready to go home? You're looking a bit flustered from the dancing," says Scott. "I have had enough. The evening has been refreshing. A good night's rest is what I need," Huli says.

Chapter 18

In the morning, Scott wakes with something soft and fluffy draped across his face. Lying beside him is Huli with her head at his feet, also finding it strange he had slept so well with her tail on his face.

Scott notices Huli's tail has a pleasant scent of a meadow laden with flowers.

Holding her tail to his nose Scott inhales the scent her tail is giving.

As he's enjoying Huli's tail, Scott sees Huli staring at him. "What are you doing?" Huli asked. "I'm sorry. I could not help myself,your tail smells nice," explained Scott.

"I am not angry with you; watching you put my tail to your noise startled me. I hope you are not angry with me crawling beside you. I wanted to be near you," Huli says.

Sitting up, Scott caresses Huli's face. "I'm not angry with you. I realize you're more woman than fox sometimes," Scott kisses Huli. A pair of eyes look into Scott's eyes not with surprise but want.

Scott reciprocates Huli's desires by embracing her with another a passionate kiss.

Huli does not speak; her heart is pounding with excitement. "You know if we are to continue, it could be a problem in the future. Your punishment could end, and you'll return to your homeland." Scott says " We can deal with that issue when it happens." replied Huli.

Scott looks at his watch. "Shit, I know someone who will be angry if we don't hurry and get to work. We'll be late as it is," Scott says.

"I promise not to get angry when women speak to you," Huli tells Scott. "It's o.k. to get a little jealous as long as you know you're the one I want to be with,"

It's near noon, and Mei Lin is preparing to open the restaurant when she hears a knock at her door.

"We're not open yet. Wait for another ten minutes!" Mei Lin shouts.

Miss, I am not here for the food; this is the police. I need to speak to you," the office informs Mei Lin.

Unlocking the front door, Lin greets the office. "How can I help you?" "I am inquiring about an event in the neighborhood three days ago," the officer asked.

One look at the police officer; red flags start to pop up. Having worked in her grandmother's restaurant for many years, she knew most about the police, this one she had never met.

Another red flag is how he's dressed; even the crooked cops are well dressed, this one's pants are too short, and she can see his socks.

The final red flag is the partially covered gang tattoo she can see on his wrist. Scott's advice comes to mind; give them what they want. She intends to, but vaguely.

"You said three days ago something happened," Mei Lin says. "Yes. I am trying to discover the identity of the person who attacked the three

men. Can you remember if you served anyone during the hours between one and three o'clock that afternoon?"

"Between one and three, you say. Let's see if I can remember. It was a slow day, an elderly couple, one of your police officers, and I remember a man and woman stuffing themselves," Mei Lin says. "The man, and woman, do you know them? Can you describe what they look like?"

Lin becomes creative in describing Scott and Huli.

"The man, I don't know his name, but he eats here occasionally. He's about a

couple of inches taller than you with brown hair. The woman I had never seen before. She's shorter than me with long black hair; they paid in cash. That is all I can remember, officer," Mei Lin described. "That's fine, Miss Lin. You have helped a lot," the phony office says.

As soon as Mei Lin is alone, she places a call to the police station, remembering what Scott told her about O'Malley; he was an honest police officer.

The sergeant at the desk answers Mei Lin's call. "Orlando Police, how can I help you?" "Hello, I am the owner of the Happy Dragon restaurant; I would like to speak to officer O'Malley if he is in," "You're in luck; he hasn't left for his patrol yet. I'll get him."

"Officer O'Malley, how can I help you?". "Listen carefully; My name is Mei Lin; I'm the owner of the Happy Dragon. I wish to invite you to an important dinner on behalf of Mr. Glassman. He informed me you are an honest policeman if you take the hint. I will see you here in an hour, thank you," Mei Lin hangs up abruptly.

"What did the woman want?" the sergeant asked O'Malley. "Someone dumped trash over her front lawn. She wants me to look

into it. Yeah, like that's going to happen. It's a job for trash removal. I'll give them a call later," O'Malley says.

Officer O'Malley makes a detour to the Happy Dragon during his patrol. "It's nice to see you're punctual," Lin says, greeting O'Malley. "I'm here, so what's the problem?"

Chapter 19

"Have a seat; lunch is on me while we talk. Someone we are both acquainted with is in danger. Earlier today, someone poorly dressed excuse for a policeman paid me a visit asking about Mr.Glassman. Scott told me if Angel's men confront me, tell them what they want to hear, not to put my life in danger.

I did and didn't tell the idiot what he wanted to hear, giving you time to ask Scott to run.

My description of Scott and Huli wasn't very accurate. Angel is not an idiot; he will discover Scott is the person who trashed his men," Mei Lin explains.

"I thank you for this news, Miss Lin. As soon as I leave here, I will visit him at his workplace," Officer O'Malley assures her.

"Is there a chance of you protecting him, especially Huli? She is more special than you could imagine," Mei Lin asked.

"I'm afraid not. Too few of those like me, "O'Malley tells Mei Lin. "I wish you luck getting him out of the city," remarked Mie Lin.

You're a little late."Bilx says, "Yes, we are." replies Huli walking by the manager with a smile. "What's with Huli? She acting very happy," Bilx asked. "We are officially dating."

"It's nice to be young. To celebrate your relationship, how about I give you and Huli the day off with pay?" "You don't have to, Mr.Bilx," Scott insisted. "I insist. I believe in rewarding love," Bilx quotes.

"Huli, since we have the day to ourselves, let's enjoy it with a walk around Lake Eola, " Scott suggested. Huli's smile signals she's looking forward to Scott's suggestion.

The short work day will start events that will change Huli and Scott's lives.

The air is excellent on a late autumn day, with low humidity, making it a perfect day for a walk holding hands.

During their walk, officer O'Malley stops by Scott's workplace. "Is Mr.Glassman here?" officer O'Malley asked Mr.Bilx. "No, I gave him the day off. Is he in trouble with the law?" Bilx asked. "Not exactly. He might be in danger. Is the woman he's with here?" O'Malley asked. "No. Huli is with Mr. Glassman." "Do you know where they are?" O'Malley asked. "I think I heard them mention taking a walk around Lake Eola," Bilx tells O'Malley. "Thank you for your help Mr. Bilx."

Scott and Huli are finishing their walk around the lake; Scott suggests that they walk to the Happy Dragon.

Usually, he would take the bus because of the heat and humidity, but today's weather is very refreshing they walk.

"Mei Lin's description of Scott and Huli of the assault on Angel's men does not buy Scott much time. As Scott said to Mei Lin, she is a poor liar. Cho's intimidation of the locals

revealed that Scott and Huli were in that alley that day.

The two love birds are non the wiser of the threat to them until some Angel's men block their way.

"Huli, get behind me!" Scott says. "It won't protect her," Angel says, standing behind them with fifty of his thugs at his side.

Scott turns to see Angel raising a gun; instinctively, pushing Huli away, the weapon rings out.

Taking Huli's hand, Scott runs down an alley.

"Shall we give chase?" Cho asked Angel. "We will; there's no rush since it's a dead-end where they are going. Besides, I didn't

miss him. All we need to do is follow the trail of blood," Angel states.

Scott realizes he has made a mistake when he discovers he and Huli are trapped.

Even if he could escape, it's too late. The bullet went through his kidney, and he's bleeding to death.

Scott falls to the ground. "Huli, there's a fire escape ladder for you to escape. I know you're agile enough to get out of here before they arrive,"

"No, you are coming with me!" Huli says. "I can't. The bullet found its mark," Scott tells her,

removing his blood-stained hand from his side.

Huli grasps Scott's bloody hand. "No!" she cries out.

The feel, the smell of Scott's blood, has Huli's heart pound with a vengeance and something she has never felt in the past, fear. The overwhelming fear of losing something or one precious.

Huli's heart pounds so much that she clenches her chest.

"Huli, are you right?" Scott asked. She stares at Scott with fiery red eyes. "I will save you. Do not move," says Huli as she calmly walks toward Angel and his men.

Chapter 20

Cho points out he sees Huli walking toward them.

Huli's body is emanating with a red glow of anger. Her ears and nine tails are visible. The closer Huli got to Angel, the more her body reverted to her proper form. Finally, standing before Angel, Cho, and their gang is a white nine-tail fox twice the size of a tiger.

"A cheap trick is not going to save you," Angel shouts.

Cho's reaction is much different from Huli's appearance. "Boss, we should get out of here," Cho says, trembling with fear. "You can't be frightened by a cheap magic trick," Angel tells Cho.

"Boss, that thing should not exist. I'm leaving!" Cho says, sprinting away. His exit is too little to late.

Before Angel could shoot Cho for running, his body burst into flames.

Foxfire can turn any living thing to ashes. Huli's love for Scott turned her fire into much more; not only did Cho's body become ashes, but she devoured his soul.

"What the hell!" Angel shouts.

"No one is leaving here alive," Huli remarked.

"You damn bitch!" Angel wheels his body to shoot Huli, only to find his arm with the gun is missing.

" Aargh!!!" Angel cries out in pain. In front of Angel, Huli has the missing arm in her mouth. Spitting it out, she says. "You will be the last to go,"

Angel commands his people. "Kill that thing! Shoot it!"

Lying in a pool of blood at the back of the alley, Scott hears repeated gunfire and people screaming as his senses begin to dim.

The last to feel Huli's vengeance is Angel. "No! What are you?" Angel shouts. "Retribution," Huli replies as she incinerates him.

Huli rushes back to Scott. "I have returned to save you!" Huli says. "I'm afraid it's too late; my time has come. At least I get to see how beautiful you are before I die. I'm sorry I could not spend more time with you.... It's getting dark; I'm cold; maybe in the next life, we'll meet."

Scott's life slips away.

"Nooo! You cannot leave me! I finally learned what love is; I love you!"

Desperation, sadness, and fear prompt Huli's mind to go beyond ordinary thinking. She turns her head to look at her tails. It takes her a split second to do what must be done. Grasping one of her tails with her teeth, she rips it from her body.

Laying it on Scott's still body, Huli's flame flows through him.

"I pray your soul has not left. Please return to me," Huli pleads. Then, as her tail fades, Scott's chest rises as he takes a breath.

"You live, thank the Gods!" Huli exclaims. Scott's eyes open. "I'm alive. The pain is gone. Huli, what did you do?" Scott asked.

"She did the unthinkable," a voice says. "Lie Gong, is that you?" Huli asked. "It is. Scott Glassman, what Huli did to save you is unimaginable for her species. Not only did she sacrifice one of her tails, but she also did it for the love of a human. Huli has sacrificed her perfection as a spirit fox.

What do you have to say for your self Huli Jing?" Lie Gong says. "I do not have to give you a reason. It was my choice to make." Huli remarked.

Reaching for Huli's face, Scott says. "You should not have sacrificed your tail for me. I will live for another fifty years at best, and your tail will be gone forever,"

"Scott Glassman, your life will exist longer than you think.

Each tail on a spirit fox is the culmination of power and time. Huli gave you one of her tails; doing so extended your life a thousand years or two." Lie Gong informs Scott.

"If that's the case, it looks like Huli and I will have plenty of

time getting to know and love each other."

Scott can hear people entering the alley, curious about the gunshots.

"Huli, we can discuss our next move after we leave this place. The gunfire I heard will attract even the crooked cops. I assume you killed Angel and his gang. I don't want to explain why there are so many dead bodies," Scott states." "Dead yes, bodies no. No one will find them." Huli says.

"Mr.Glassman, if you wish to leave, Huli can take you anywhere in the world. That is one of her perks, giving you her tail," Lie Gong says. "If we can

travel anywhere. I'd like to visit your home Huli."

Chapter 21

Before we go, I would like to make a couple of pit stops." Scott requested.

At the Happy Dragon, Mei Lin is in the back store room when Scott appears behind her.

"Hi Mei Lin," says Scott startling her. "Damn you, Glassman, you scared the crap out of me! It would be best if you were not here. Angel will find you," Mei Lin warns him.

"Angel and his men won't harm anyone. Huli and I stopped over

to say goodbye," "Goodbye? Where's Huli?" Mei Lin asked.

Entering the room, Lin cannot believe what she is seeing. The glow of Huli's proper form brightens the dark room.

Tears flow from Lin's eyes as she falls to her knees.

Scott doesn't know how to react when Mei Lin begins to cry like a baby.

Huli walks over to Lin so that she can touch her. "Is this a normal reaction when women see you as a fox?" Scott asked Huli. "How would I know? I never allowed anyone to see me.

Give me a moment to deal with Lin and her family," Huli says to

Scott. "Family? Lin is the only one here," Scott replies.

There are two; one wiping her nose on my fur and the other lingering," says Huli.

"Cease your crying child, and stop wiping your nose on my fur. Scott and I will be returning to my homeland soon," Huli tells Lin. "Where is that?" Lin asked. China, near or at the Jainca County temple," Huli tells her.

"How is Scott supposed to accompany you?" Mei Lin asked. You don't have to worry about me; I'm no longer human," says Scott.

Huli looks up at the ceiling. "Now that you have seen me, it's time for you to pass on. There's a better world waiting for you," Huli says. "Who are you speaking to?' Mei Lin asked. "Your grandmother. She's been hanging around watching you and wanting to see me," Huli says.

"Mei Lin, we have to go. Huli and I need to make one more stop before going to China," says Scott.

"Before you leave, Huli, do you understand what love is?" Lin asked her. "I do. As you said, It can be as painful as it is wonderful. Love is now part of the natural order of my life," Huli answered.

A flame circled Scott and Huli; at that moment, they vanished.

There's a knock on Bren's door. "Coming, I'll be right there," replies Scott's sister. Opening the door, she finds her brother and Huli standing.

"Scott! Huli!!! Is that you?" "It is I," Huli replied. "Come in! I don't want people to see her." Bren says. "You do not have to be concerned about other people seeing me. I am allowing you to see me in this form," Huli says. "Seeing you like this means you're leaving," Bren says. "We are, Sis. We're here to say goodbye, and you can do what

you want with my stuff," Scott tells his sister.

"I can't even comprehend how you're going to travel. What I need to know; Are you happy?" Bren asked her brother. "We are. China is not that far away for someone like Huli. When we're settled down, we might pop in for a visit now and then," Scott explained.

"I wish the two of you well. Huli, for some reason, seeing you makes my heart feel warm inside." Bren says. "She has that effect on women," Scott remarked. "Have a good trip," Bren gives Huli and her brother a kiss and hugs before they

disappear in the ball of flame.

Chapter 22

Scott and Huli return to China outside the Jaina temple. "Wow! That was awesome," exclaimed Scott.

Witnessing Scott's arrival is the monk Bea Sung. "Who are you? How did you get here?"

Scott paused replying because he was surprised, he understand the monk's language. He was more surprised when he could reply. "Forgive me. My name is Scott Glassman; I came here with Huli Jing."

"Huli! Where is she?" the monk asked. "I'm over here, monk,"

Bea Sung turns around, looking up face to face at Huli.

"Scott let me introduce you to Bea Sung; he is the monk who runs this temple. Mr.Sung looks at Huli and then Scott.

"Mr.Sung, Huli is not here to cause trouble, we can clear the your confusion over a cup of tea," Scott suggested.

One hour later, Scott, Huli, and Bea Sung are outside the temple.

"Mr.Glassman, that is an amazing story. I would never have thought Huli would fall in love. Your life with Huli will be an eternity. Have you thought what that might feel like?" Bea Sung asked.

"Mr. Sung, I look at it this way; We can have a lot of fun getting to know each other in an eternity," Scott stated.

Sung is surprised by Huli's expression; she's blushing.

"So, what are your plans?" Sung asked Scott. "This place is Huli's home. We'll be hanging around here. Do a little traveling once in a while. I have a lot to learn about my new persona, first."

One of the problems Scott will have to confront living in China are the two Chinese soldiers pointing their weapons at him.

"Raise your hands!" one of the soldiers commands. "Relax, I'm

not here to harm anyone," Scott tells the guards. "Shut up! Do not speak!" the guards commanded Scott.

"Please, lower your weapons; you are going to anger my wife," Scott pleads.

Mr. Sung rushes to Scott's aide. "If you lower your guns, I can explain why he is here." Sung' s words fall on empty ears. He has pushed to the ground." Stay on the ground, monk. I will deal with you next."

"Where is the bitch you say is your wife? We need to arrest her as well." says one of the guards.

"Now you've done it. My wife is pissed." Scott states. Huli reveals

herself, lowering her head between the guards from behind as she speaks.

"A bitch am I! Do I look like a dog to you?" Staring into Huli's fiery eyes paralyzes the guards with fear.

"Please, don't harm them, my love. They will be harmless once I relieve them of these guns." Easing over to the guards, Scott relieves the guards of their weapons.

Huli walks over to Scott. "Gentlemen, let me introduce you to the love of my life. You may have heard stories about a spirit fox that roams this area. You're looking at her; she is called Huli Jing.

Now that you're calm, I'll return your guns. I need you to contact your superiors so we can discuss my presence in your country. You do not have to worry about me leaving; I'm not going anywhere. If you want to, you can take a picture of us to convince your superiors were real," Scott suggested.

A week passes before an entourage of soldiers accompanying a single man arrives at the temple. "Mr. President Wei, it's a pleasure to meet you," Scott greets the leader of China.

"You speak my language well for an American," Wei says. "I speak many languages because of who my mate is," Scott states.

"Where is this creature?" President Wise asked. "Mr. President, please show her some respect. Her name is Huli Jing," Scott requested.

Dictators are proud, and President Wei did not like Scott, insisting he gives Huli respect. Instead inserting his authority, Wei swallowed his pride on a better part of caution.

"Huli, can you come here? The President of China wishes to speak to you," Scott calls out.

Huli walking from the temple in her human form does not impress President Wei.

"Is she the fox in the picture?" We asked Scott. "It's her. Huli can change into whatever form she wishes," Scott explained.

"Huli, I think President Wei wants to see how beautiful you are," Scott says. She transforms into her animal form.

"Is this grand enough for you?" If you call me a bitch I'll eat you," Huli says. "President Wei stares at Huli and then the two soldiers who patrol this area. "We did not know who she was, Mr. President," Zhou said.

"Can I touch you?" Wei asked Huli. "Go ahead," she replies.

Stroking her fur for a second causes the President to step away. "You're real!" Wei shouts. "Of course I am," Huli says.

President Wei steps away to speak to his generals in private.

Scott observes Wei speaking to his subordinates. He has seen enough underhanded people talking where he came from to know the President is planning to do something ill-advised.

"President Wei, excuse me if I am blunt with this warning. My wife will not take it well if you intend to harm me. You have no

idea what she is capable of doing.

If you attempted to harm her, I have enough knowledge and power to send your country to the stone age.

Can I make a suggestion?" Scott asked. "I will listen," Wei replied.

"Think of all the money on tourism you can make when people visit to see her. Also, Huli affects people near her, as you noticed. She brings out the goodness in people. Your country could be known as the land of enlightenment. Huli can be very beneficial to you and your country,"

"Mr. Glassman, your proposition sounds wonderful, except you are not of China. You do not look like you are from my country. It could cause an issue with those in my government," Wei states.

"I understand my presence might cause problems; give me a moment with my wife.

Huli, is it possible for me to change into a fox?" Scott asked her.

Chapter 23

"With my help, you could. Take hold of my hand; I want you to imagine yourself as a fox." Huli instructs Scott.

Scott's body starts to glow as his body transforms into a fox.

"This is awesome! How do I look, Huli?" Scott asked. "You look like the handsome fox I love," she replies.

"Um? Red fur. My size is more significant than an ordinary fox. President Wei, will this do? I'm

not a native fox of China, but a fox I am.

I will remain as a fox when people are in the area and human when Huli and I are alone."

President Wei holds out his hand. "Welcome to my country Mr. Glassman," Scott places his paw on Wei's hand. "It's a pleasure being here. There's one thing I need to mention, Huli and I do not talk politics, and the monk will deal with religion," Scott stipulates. President Wei nods in agreement.

"Once it gets out that we are here, you will need people for crowd control. I can suggest the

two guards who spoke to me earlier. They are familiar with the area," says Scott. "I will keep that in mind, Mr.Glassman," Wei says.

"Also, I will change my name to fit my persona. When Huli and I decide what it will be, I will pass it on to the monk to inform you," Scott says.

A year passes, Huli's fame explodes, and people from all over the world visit her and Scott at the temple.

Three familiar faces arrive at the temple steps, and Scott is there to greet them. "Hi, Bren. Mei Lin and officer O'Malley, nice to see you,"

They look around to see who's speaking to them. "Scott, is that you? Where are you?" Bren asked.

"Look at the base of the temple pillar," replied Scott. A large curled mound of reddish fur stands up. "Can you see me now?" Scott says.

"Scott is that you!" his sister shouts. "Not so loud. Yes, it's me. So what you're seeing is my other persona, thanks to Huli. I have to remain like this in public. At the request of the Chinese government, a fox in public and human in private. Welcome to China."

"Can I touch you?" Bren asked. "Go ahead," Scott says. "You're real." "What, you couldn't believe your eyes." Scott states. "Where's Huli?" Mei Lin asked. "She's resting in the temple." "Bren, I see you, and officer O'Malley are holding hands," noticed Scott.

"It's captain O'Malley, thanks to Huli, I suspect. Your sister and I met at your apartment; one thing led to another," O'Malley explained. "Congratulations, may you and my sister have a happy life," Scott says.

Scott's conversation is cut short by Huli's cry for help.

"Scott! Come here. I need you! Something has happened."

Scott, Bren, Mei Lin, and O'Malley rush into the temple, where they find a pleasant surprise for them and a big one for Huli.

Lying on the floor, Huli raises her head, revealing two newborn white kit foxes.

"Huli, why didn't you say you were pregnant?" Scott asked. "I did not know I was. I felt a little tired; this should not happen," exclaimed Huli.

"They're adorable, Huli," Lin states. "To you maybe, but I do not give birth to young foxes.

Lie Gong, is this you're doing?" Huli calls out. The statue of Buddha on the alter begins to glow.

"It is not Lei Gong Huli. You are in my house; I believe your love deserves a reward.

They have the gift to heal the soul. Love and protect them; they will be vulnerable their first year." "What do I know about raising young is kits," Huli says. "You will do fine, Huli. Whether fox or human, you are female. Instinct and love, with Scott at your side, a good mother you will be, Huli."

The statue's glow fades, and Huli and Scott Nussle their beautiful wonders.

"Can they speak?" Lin asked. "Not for a few centuries; they must mature in spiritual strength," Huli says.

"Huli, I have to speak to the guards in charge of this area. The Buddha left us with a cryptic warning about our children. There may be those who do not wish for our children to live for one reason or another," says Scott.

Chapter 24

"Mr. Wang, Mr. Zhou, can you follow me? I need to show you something," Scott says to the guards.

The two guards follow Scott to the temple, where their motions freeze when they see Huli's kits.

"Now you know why I called you here. The deity of this temple gave the kits as a gift. They are exceptional, and with that came a warning. There will be an ungodly amount of people coming to see them, and some may wish to harm them because

of what they can do," Scott tells Zhou and Wang.

"What can they do?" Zhou asked. "We were told they can heal the soul. That's why I need you to contact your superiors. You will need more security to protect the children for their first year," Scott explained. "The two guards took Scott's warning seriously. Anything with Huli and those associated with her is considered a national treasure. The seriousness of the guards' health is at risk if Huli or her kits are injured.

Scott returned to the temple, where Bren and Lin are speaking with Huli.

"How's life in Orlando?" Scott asked O'Malley. "More peaceful after your sweetheart disposed of about seventy problems that gave the city of Orlando a bad name. It was nice of Huli to leave Angel's arm behind so that we could identify him at least," O'Malley remarked.

"I assure you, Captian O'Malley, it wasn't intentional; she had other problems weighing on her mind at the time.

"How long are you visiting?" Scott asked. "We were staying for two days. It was Mei Lin who paid for our trip.

Are you happy where you're at?"O'Malley asked Scott. "Very happy," Scott replied.

The birth of the kits has the Chinese government taking no chances with the security of the temple and its occupants.

An increase in tourists prompted more guards to be more visible.

As a spirit fox, Huli keeps many secrets to herself, particularly her connection to the land; a group of unwanted guests is about to find out.

From a sound sleep with her kits, Huli's head rises up in anger. "Huli, what is it?" Scott asked.

"Fanatical blood lust has entered this country. A large group of people are heading towards us from the north," says Huli. "Do you know where north?" Scott asked. "Near the Juan Basin," Huli says. "Too bad you could be more specific where they are; I could lead the military to stop them," Scott remarks.

"I can, since you are part of me," Huli says. "Perfect. I want you to stay close to our children; the temple will be closed until the threat has been dealt with," Scott tells Huli.

Scott hurries to find one of the original guards, Zhou, to inform him of the danger.

"Zhou!!" Scott shouts to get his attention. "Why are you shouting?" Zhou inquired. "Listen carefully; I need you to contact your President, before you ask why I'll tell you. Huli has sensed a large group of people entering your country with much blood lust. Huli knows they are heading here to kill our children.

Contact who you need so I can lead you to them. At the moment, the enemy is at the Juan Basin." Scott informs Zhou.

Chapter 25

"I want you to be careful; you are not immortal as I am. You can die if your body is too badly damaged," Huli warns Scott. "Do me a favor, change to a human," asked Scott.

Taking Huli in his arms, he gives her a passionate kiss. "Having two legs does have benefits," Scott says. "I agree, " Huli replied.

"I promise to come back. An eternity without you and the children is too terrifying to consider; I love you. If you get a little bored, you could think of

names for the children and me. The Chinese government has been nagging me for a name,"

Scott leaves with Zhou and a contingent of elite Chinese soldiers.

"It's been three days since Scott's departure, and the only human interaction Huli is having is with the temple monk Bea Sung.

"You look worried. You miss your mate," Sung states. "I do, but that does not worry me. I sense something has happened to him. That idiot love of mine is reckless in his actions. I warned him to be cautious," "I'm sure he will be safe. I'm certain Buddha

is protecting him," Sung consoled Huli.

It's no surprise to Huli when Scott returns to the temple; what is are Zhou's reaction toward her? He kneels before she gives her thanks.

"What is wrong with him?" Huli asked Scott. "He's thankful for you saving his life," replied Scott. "When did I save his life?" remarked Huli.

"When I took the impact of a grenade to protect him, he started to praise me like he's doing to you. I told him it was you that saved his life," Scott says.

"Don't you think I have enough people thanking me? You take the credit for this human.

Something else happened; what is it?" Huli inquired.
"Nothing gets by you. Something did happen to me when I saved Zhou's life,"

Scott transforms into a fox; instead of a red fox, he is twice the size, all white, and has two tails.

"How do I look? It seems I have leveled up," says Scott. "It seems you have, your more handsome than ever," Huli remarked.

" How are the kids doing?"
"They are fine and rambunctious.

I am finding it difficult keeping them locked up in this temple." "It should be o.k. to let them run around; no one will harm them. The Chinese government knows who's behind the attack. Our biggest problem will be the crowds getting too close to the children." Scott says. "I can keep them hidden from human eyes. The public will view them under my supervision tells Scott.

"When they are old enough to be on their own, you and I will do some traveling. The monk can act as a babysitter." Scott suggested. "I would like that," Huli says.

"Have you decided what to call our kids?" Scott asked.

"You will be called Bohai, powerful sea wave. The female will be Chenric, amazing morning, and the male Bolin, gentle rain." "They are beautiful names like their mother," Scott says, kissing Huli.

The End

Huli

Publication through Amazon

You can find many more short stories from this author on Amazon.

I dedicate this book to my loving wife Joyce, who has been at my side for many years and I hope for many more.

www.ingramcontent.com/pod-product-compliance
Lightning Source LLC
LaVergne TN
LVHW050542160826
845677LV00011B/2137

* 9 7 9 8 8 4 4 3 2 3 0 6 5 *